MONTANA WARRIOR

HEIRS OF GUARDIAN VALLEY

BOOK TWO

HALLIE BENNETT

I0619501

Searching for more protective heroes?
Check out the Mountain Men of
Suitor's Crossing series <u>here</u>[1]!

---

1. https://www.amazon.com/Protected-Mountain-Man-Romance-Crossing-ebook/dp/B0BNM2M6RY

CHAPTER ONE

SAMANTHA MANNING

"I know most of the men in Guardian Valley, and no one, I mean no one, meets the description of this freaking lumberjack."

THIS IS A STUPID IDEA. A stupid, reckless idea. But it's too late to turn back now. Too late to let my brother—a former Marine—handle whatever awaits me at the top of this damn mountain.

Okay, so not quite a mountain, but a freaking big hill. One that I was not prepared to hike this morning after last night's festivities, AKA my brother and sister-in-law's belated wedding reception/baby shower.

But I was still feeling a little sad—a little restless—after watching them dance and laugh and be so freaking adorable together. Who'd have thought my big gruff brother would find love with such a sweet woman like Adeline?

Would fall in love and get married before me? Heath's hopeless romantic little sister?

I sigh as the secluded cabin I'm headed toward comes into view. It's a cute little house settled on a ledge that juts into the river, rushing water running by two sides of it. The sunrises are gorgeous if you happen to be sitting out on the porch at just the right time.

But I haven't been up here in forever. The trek from the main house through the woods has my body huffing and puffing for air.

"Just one peek then turn around," I tell myself.

I don't know what possessed me to choose this as my morning task to shake those pesky insecurities of being alone forever. Heath said it looked like someone had been up here in passing. He definitely didn't mean for me to go check it out.

It's probably a rogue hunter who wandered onto our land—or rather Adeline's land since a dead billionaire CEO bequeathed it to her after our dad sold the ranch. Or maybe a lost hiker, though we probably would've heard about that on the news.

It could be a serial killer for all I knew. A killer on the lam, searching for his next victim. Preferably a brunette with extra curves and no dating prospects.

Time to lay off the true crime docs, girl.

But something was drawing me up here to find out what was going on for myself. Like I said: a stupid, reckless—

The smartest damn thing I've ever done in my life.

The sound of an ax splitting through a log rings through the air, and after cresting a ridge of rocks, I spy a man through the thicket of trees. A giant, really. Drenched in sweat and wielding a giant-ass ax overhead before swinging it down with a grunt.

Holy cow.

My pussy clenches instinctually as my hand falls to the tree trunk in front of me, nails digging into the rough bark.

Who the hell is that?

I know most of the men in Guardian Valley, and no one, I mean *no one*, meets the description of this freaking lumberjack.

Rippling muscles bulge beneath his tan skin. Skin that's covered in ragged scars, bright pink across his back and shoulders. Short blonde hair glints under the sun, and I desperately need him to turn around so I can see his face.

No doubt accompanied by a massive chest heaving with his exertion.

Oh god. Is it possible to come just from watching a hot stranger chop wood? Because the longer I stare, the harder it becomes to breathe and the damper my panties get.

Alright, Samantha, you've got this. How does one approach the living embodiment of every wet dream they've ever had?

Hey, stranger! Mind if I ass you a question?

My eyes skim down his torso to where his jeans rest over his hips and firm butt. Yeah, no, I don't want to creep him out with puns about body parts. Especially body parts I'm ogling from afar like a horny spinster desperate to be tossed over his shoulder and—

Oh, wait... That's exactly what I am.

It's your family's land, or it used to be, or it is again since Heath married Adeline. Honestly, the ownership of the ranch has exchanged hands so much lately, it's a miracle I don't have whiplash.

Either way—Heath's or Adeline's—this stranger has no cause to be here. Chopping down our trees and looking damn good doing it. So, I'm just going to march over there and demand he tell me what the heck he's doing here. There's probably a perfectly logical explanation, and once that's taken care of, we can move on to more pressing matters.

Like the lusty devil currently residing on my shoulder.

"Take a picture, it'll last longer," a male voice calls out, the throwback insult from middle school jarring me out of my spiraling. "And while you're at it, you can get the hell off my land."

His land?

CHAPTER TWO

DEREK HOUSELY

"Looking like an overstuffed scarecrow with bulging seams doesn't exactly cause panties to drop."

MONTANA SUITS ME.

Desolate. Cold. Free from hordes of people who look at me with either pity or horror.

Since surviving the plane crash that killed my dad and eight other people—leaving me as the only survivor at thirteen years old—most folks call me *lucky*. My social worker Nancy. Every foster family I lived with. From the terrible to the okay.

How fortunate you were so young!

You were meant to live!

I've heard it all. When I joined the Army and the guys found out about my past, even then I was dubbed Lucky Charm.

As if the multiple surgeries and skin grafts I had meant nothing. As if the scars marring sixty percent of my body were invisible.

Some days I think it would've been easier if I'd died with my dad rather than continue breathing as a fucking beast.

Breathing.

Because I sure as hell wasn't living.

But thanks to good ole Mr. Foster, the CEO of the company my dad worked for, the reason we'd been on that fateful plane, I don't have to deal with anyone else's bullshit anymore.

I punched my ticket out of the military three months ago and walked from Fayetteville, North Carolina all the way to Guardian Valley, Montana. The trip kept me focused. Gave me time to adjust back to civilian life.

And now I'm ready to settle into my new inherited home. Let the rest of the heirs live in the main house and cabins, but this rustic little shack away from everyone else is mine.

Suddenly, the air changes around me. The casual chatter of the forest has disappeared.

I'm not alone. Someone's out here. Spying on me.

"Take a picture, it'll last longer," I shout. "And while you're at it, you can get the hell off my land."

"You've got it wrong, mister. This is my family's land."

I don't know what I was expecting. But the defiant feminine tone of my spy isn't it. Throwing the ax down with more force than necessary, I turn to face my unwanted visitor and gape in shock at the beautiful woman before me.

Where the hell did she come from?

"Hate to break it to you, gorgeous, but this land belongs to me. You can check with my lawyer, Mr. Tan."

"Oh, I know all about Mr. Tan," she says, swaggering closer, her round hips drawing my attention past her lush breasts and soft belly. "You must be one of Mr. Foster's heirs."

"I am," I confirm.

"Well, what he failed to share was that the first person to arrive at Serenity Ranch received the deed to the land and all of the buildings. And you, mister, are late. Mrs. Adeline Manning, formerly Croup, is the proud owner of Serenity Ranch along with my brother, her husband."

What the hell?

There's no reason for the woman to lie to me, but I don't know what that means for my status at this cabin.

"The will said that we would all be able to stay on the property. That should still hold true even if this Adeline holds the deed."

The woman bites her lip, then reluctantly nods. "You're right. But you'll understand if we confirm your identity first, right? Anyone could have heard about the inheritance and decided to claim part of this land as theirs."

"I'm no squatter."

"That remains to be seen." She smirks, winking at me.

"Why were you skulking around out here?" I ask, changing the subject because I'm not about to run inside and grab my ID for this little slip of a woman.

"My brother mentioned some inconsistencies here at the cabin. Thought I would check it out for him."

"Your brother's okay with that?" What kind of man lets his little sister roam through the wilderness alone? Confronting men without proper backup?

"Well, he doesn't exactly know," she admits.

"Why doesn't that surprise me? You seem like the type to do what she wants and fuck the consequences."

"You don't even know me."

"I've met enough women." It's an unfair judgment of her. A dick move. But her sass tempts me to do something I'll regret—her sexy curves, too.

Steam's practically rising from my overheated skin from the workout of chopping firewood, and now I've got this beautiful stranger turning up the temperature in my blood to fucking molten. Which is pathetic because I'm a thirty-three year old virgin for a reason.

Looking like an overstuffed scarecrow with bulging seams doesn't exactly cause panties to drop.

And pinched expressions of pity don't exactly make my dick hard either.

Those are the only two reactions I receive from women: disgust or pity. So, I've grown content with my cock in one hand and a romance novel in the other.

The guys in my unit used to laugh when they caught me reading Christine Feehan or Lora Leigh. They downright guffawed at the sight of a historical romance with windswept heroines and Fabio lookalikes.

But I took it in stride because they didn't know what they were missing. One of the nicer foster moms I had kept a collection of romances, and once when I was being too much of a hellion, she sat me in the living room, tossed *Beast* by Judith Ivory into my lap, and the rest was history.

Girls didn't blush or flirt around me in school, but between the pages of a book, men who bore scars like me landed the damsel in distress. Earned her love.

It's the closest I'll ever get to having a woman of my own. So, I read romances unapologetically. And jerk off to the vision of me and a mystery heroine.

"I'm going to pretend you didn't just insult an entire gender based on what appears to be very limited experience," the woman huffs, crossing her arms over her chest. "I'll let Adeline and

Heath know you're here, and we'll confirm your details with Mr. Tan, if that's alright with you."

"Fine by me." The sooner she leaves, the quicker my body temperature will return to normal. "Derek Housely. My dad was Justin Housely and worked for Mr. Foster before he died in the plane crash."

She nods, her indignant stance softening. "Samantha Manning... I'm sorry about your dad. Mine passed away recently."

I grunt in response, unsure of what to say, because what I want to do is wrap her in my arms and erase the sadness in her eyes. A wholly ridiculous reaction and bound to be an unwelcome one.

Turning my back on her, I pick up the ax again and continue splitting the pile of logs beside me into firewood. Samantha stands silent for another minute before I hear the sound of her retreating footsteps crunching through the fallen leaves and twigs littering the forest floor.

For the first time since she arrived, I'm able to breathe easier, my chest releasing the tight ache that had formed the moment I saw her.

CHAPTER THREE

SAMANTHA

"He's just going to live out there like Bear Grylls?"

DEREK NEVER CAME DOWN from the cabin.

I thought once I told Heath about his presence—and bore the brunt of my brother's overprotective lecture about wandering alone in the woods without warning anyone of my plans—that Derek would move into the main house like Adeline did when she first arrived.

The possibility had me scrubbing every surface like my life depended on it and baking cookies, muffins, pies like the spring bake sale was right around the corner. I wanted the house to be warm and welcoming for Derek, despite our initial meeting that resulted in me stomping down the mountain in a fit of anger.

"Are you sure you made it clear that he's welcome to stay here? That you and I are residing in a separate home?" Adeline asks for the third time as we finish eating breakfast.

Heath had visited Derek the same afternoon I discovered our surprise guest. I expected him to return with the gruff lumberjack in tow, but no such luck.

"Yes, sweetheart. But he made it very clear that he's happy where he is. He said the cabin suits him." My brother shrugs like it's no big deal while Adeline and I share a look of exasperation.

Men.

"Didn't you say the cabin doesn't have electricity? That it's little more than a glorified shack?"

Heath stuffs a forkful of scrambled eggs into his mouth and nods.

"But you're saying it suits him. No electricity. In February," Adeline says slowly as if she's explaining things to a toddler.

I bite the inside of my cheek to keep from chuckling. My new sister-in-law has come a long way from the shy woman who first showed up to Serenity Ranch, all grandma sweaters and one-word answers. Marriage to Heath—while initially worrisome to me considering how quickly it came about—seems to agree with her. Though her wardrobe still consists of comfy grandma sweaters.

But I've never seen my grumpy older brother so happy and relaxed—no matter what Addie wears.

"I didn't say it. He did." Heath leans closer to Adeline and massages the back of her neck before gently rubbing her pregnant belly with his other hand.

The intimate gesture sends my gaze skittering away, blinking back an onslaught of tears.

Such a simple act. One of care. Comfort.

Something I wish I had.

"He's used to sleeping in much more difficult situations. Like the desert under threat of an enemy ambush. He can handle sleeping on a full-sized bed next to a roaring fire. Hell, that sounds downright cozy."

Except for the full-sized bed part, I inwardly correct. Derek is a big man. He probably barely has room to roll over, let alone get *cozy*.

"What about food? Cooking? He's just going to live out there like Bear Grylls?"

Before Heath can answer, I jump in on impulse. "No, I'll bring him meals. I'd be cooking for him if he stayed here anyway."

"You shouldn't be making the trek by yourself so many times." Heath's eyes narrow in my direction. "Anything can happen out there, and the cell service sucks. Derek's a grown man. He knows how to take care of himself."

I let the topic drop as I drain the last of the coffee from my mug. Heath can think what he wants, but *I'm* going to *do* what I want.

Huh... My steps falter on my way to the kitchen sink. *Maybe Derek wasn't too far off about me, after all.*

THE HIKE TO THE CABIN isn't any easier the second time around, especially now that I'm lugging a backpack full of food for Derek. Heath might believe he should survive off of rabbits and squirrels, but not me. So I packed a canister of the stew we're having for lunch along with cornbread and chocolate chip cookies from the hoard overflowing the kitchen counters.

When I arrive at the cabin, I don't see Derek outside like last time, so I knock on the front door, hoping he can hear me over the rush of water cascading below. No one answers, so I try again, banging louder on the hardwood, but get the same response.

Maybe he's out hunting those rabbits I was thinking about earlier. Trying the door handle, I find it unlocked, and carefully step inside. It's been years since I've been up here, but things haven't changed much.

Still a bare bones room with a bed and dresser to one side and a kitchenette and bathroom to the other. Heading towards the tiny counter, I unpack my bag and set out the food. There's not exactly a fridge out here, but everything should keep until he gets back.

Once everything's laid out, I mentally prepare for the walk back, when a pad of paper and pen catch my attention. On impulse, I grab it and scribble out a note, tearing off the top sheet and resting it beside the canister of stew.

Smiling, I retreat back to the main house, wishing I could see Derek's face when he discovers my surprise gift to him.

CHAPTER FOUR

DEREK

"Look who came down the mountain. Mr. Grinch himself."

SOMEBODY'S BEEN HERE.

As soon as I step inside the cabin, a distinct fruity smell tickles my nose, and I know it's not from me.

A spread of food rests on the counter in the kitchen. *She brought me lunch?* I definitely didn't expect that. Especially after telling her brother that I was fine out here.

But of course, Samantha had to do what she wanted, and her note confirms it when I read the pretty cursive.

You were right. I do what I want. Fuck the consequences. Enjoy the cookies.

I take a bite of one of the cookies and groan. It's been a while since I've had chocolate chip baked goods. I forgot how much I love them.

The next day blueberry muffins appear with another note.

My thighs hate you by the way. It's a freaking workout getting up here. Enjoy the muffins!

I don't want her thighs to hate me. I want them to love me. Love being thrown over my shoulders while I eat Samantha's pussy.

Dream on.

The third day bears a banana bread loaf because a *guy your size needs an entire loaf to himself.* And this time she signed off by asking when I was going to stop trying to kill her by making her trek up here everyday.

Adding the note to the drawer where I've been safekeeping them, I tear off a hunk of bread like a caveman and decide to confront my persistent baker. Thirty minutes later, the clanking of pots and pans draws me to the main house's kitchen where Samantha is unloading the dishwasher.

"Well, well, well, look who came down the mountain. Mr. Grinch himself."

"Wrong month, gorgeous," I say, leaning against the kitchen island.

"But if the name still applies..."

"You need to stop coming up to the cabin. You're going to injure yourself."

"You sound like Heath." She rolls her eyes. "I've been going up there for four days now, and I've been fine."

"Well, four days is your limit. No more."

"The only way you're going to stop me from going up to the cabin is if you finally move in here, where we actually have electricity, heat, and a refrigerator. You know, basic amenities." A stack of plates goes in the overhead cabinet before she bends to grab more. The black material of her leggings stretch over her ass so tightly that I'm practically drooling at the thought of falling into that tempting seam and seeing if her pussy's as sweet as her pastries. "You inherited a frick ton of money, according to Adeline. There's no reason you should be slumming it out in that shack in the middle of winter, no less."

"I like my shack."

"It has its rustic charm. Don't get me wrong. But in the summer, when it's warmer."

"Why do you want me in this house so bad? Your brother said it's just you. Lonely?"

"Only when it comes to you." The last of the dishes are put away. She sidles closer so her breasts brush against my chest, and suddenly I'm in unfamiliar territory. Surely she's not flirting with me.

"What's that supposed to mean?"

"I... I don't know... Nothing." She blushes and looks away quickly, stepping back. "Look, now that you're here, you can do me a favor."

"What kind of favor?"

"I volunteered to help set up the rec center for a community event. We could use a guy with your muscles around."

"Me and crowds don't do well." *The understatement of the century.*

"It won't be a crowd. Come on, what were you planning on doing anyway? Stomping down here, giving me your edict, and then just escaping back up the mountain?"

"Pretty much." My arms cross over my chest. The epitome of stubborn and defiant.

Samantha continues as if she didn't hear me, "You've been alone for too long. It's time to join the community."

"I like being alone," I retort.

"Spoken like someone who's truly never found the place they belong."

I ignore the ache in my chest when her guess hits home. It's true there hasn't been a sense of belonging in me for years, even my time in the military didn't lower my walls completely.

"Don't worry, I have a feeling Guardian Valley is the place for you. Besides, aren't you the least bit curious to meet Adeline, one of the other Foster heirs?"

"Don't see why I should be. What she gets doesn't affect my inheritance, and you already said she has the deed to the ranch, which is fine by me."

Samantha's eyes narrow as she huffs in frustration. "You're a tough cookie to crack."

"You're mixing your idioms. Am I a cookie or a nut? Are you trying to crack me or break me?"

"Never break. Bending might be nice, but we're getting way off track here."

Unbidden, my mind goes to bending her over the kitchen table. But I keep that to myself. "Since you're not gonna let this go, I'll help you with your volunteer event. In return, you'll agree to stop coming up to the cabin."

"No."

"I thought we were compromising."

"You might have thought that, but it was never in my plan." She grabs my arm and tugs me out to a truck.

I've got more muscle on Samantha and years of training to withstand her pushiness, but my body does nothing but follow her. As if it knows that near Samantha is where I really want to be anyway.

Even if it makes me look like a whipped puppy dog trailing after scraps of attention.

It's a twenty-minute drive through acres of land before we reach civilization. "Welcome to Guardian Valley's downtown." Samantha waves her hand towards the charming buildings gracing either side of the street.

It's not much of a downtown in the traditional sense. Not a skyscraper or backed-up traffic in sight. But there are plenty of bustling businesses with vehicles filling most of the parking spots lining the street.

"Nice," I grunt, studying the brick building Samantha parallel parks beside.

"Nice? It's downright adorable." Indignation charges her tone. Pride for her home rising to the forefront. "We could film a hit Hallmark movie on these streets, it's so darn cute."

"I'll take your word for it." I act like I've never seen a Hallmark movie in my life, but that would be a lie. Because like romance novels, cheesy TV rom-coms help me relax and imagine a happy ending for myself—even if it's fictional.

"You're gonna take more than that," she mutters as we get out of the truck and hike up the stairs of the community center. "When you move into the main house," Samantha pins me with a pointed stare, "we're watching a list of my favorites. Maybe it'll brighten your mood."

Curious as to how our tastes match up, I can't help asking what her favorites are. Maybe I've already seen what she wants to share.

"Love and Sunshine." A summer movie featuring a military veteran, a golden retriever, and a local business owner. Yeah, that's a good one.

"It's not Christmas anymore, but I own this one: Snow Bride." A gossip reporter ends up spending Christmas with a prominent political family's son.

I hold the door open for Samantha and without thinking, I say, "I like that one, too."

Samantha pauses in the middle of the hall, causing me to bump into her back. She slowly turns around. "You like that one, *too*?" Her hand forms a fist and playfully punches my arm. "So, you *do* watch Hallmark, and you *know* I'm right about Guardian Valley fitting their aesthetic perfectly. You were just messing with me."

She shakes her head in fake annoyance, a grin twitching at the corner of her lips. "You're just full of surprises, aren't you?"

With her, I guess I am.

Because I've never revealed something so personal about myself before—even if it is as inconsequential as the kinds of movies I prefer.

CHAPTER FIVE

SAMANTHA

"Could I be falling for this scarred veteran?"

"WE'RE HAPPY TO SUPPORT such a worthwhile cause, Mrs. Balducci." My back stiffens at the familiar voice coming from across the room, and a grimace forms as I confirm that my ex-boyfriend Louis is here.

Shit!

Louis and I dated for a year in high school before he left for college, and I stayed behind to help my dad on the ranch. We didn't see each other much when he returned during school breaks or after his graduation when he took a job out-of-state.

However, last year he moved back to Guardian Valley and made it obvious that he wanted to resume our previous relationship—despite it being over a decade since we last dated. I really should've turned him down, but I was lonely. My prospects were zero, and my stupid romantic heart rationalized that maybe this was how things were always meant to be.

Louis and I go our separate ways as teens, only to reunite as adults, mature and experienced, ready for a serious relationship.

What a load of crap.

Because Louis hadn't changed much from high school. He remained so forgetful it verged on neglect. At first, I thought it was charming how he'd be so focused on studying for a chemistry test or perfecting his curveball for the baseball team. He was dedicated and wasn't that a great quality to have in a boyfriend?

Except he was never dedicated to me. Not as a senior in high school and not as a thirty-something year old man.

Not that Louis saw it that way.

He gave me as much time as he could and I should be grateful for it. The memory of our breakup has my teeth grinding together. It wasn't mutual—Louis thought I'd get over my *issues* eventually—so seeing him now means I have to deal with another annoying inquiry on whether or not I've come to my senses.

Because he and I both know it's slim pickings in Guardian Valley.

But slim as they are, I'm not desperate enough to lose my self-respect by settling for Louis Meeks. Especially not with a man like Derek in proximity.

Sure, Derek doesn't seem to like me that much, and I almost admitted to my crush earlier in the kitchen when he commented on my loneliness, which would've been embarrassing, but that hasn't stopped my fantasies of winning him over.

Plus, he freaking watches Hallmark movies! That wasn't even on my bingo card for the perfect man, yet he managed to tick that box with no trouble.

"Do you know that guy?" Derek unfolds another metal chair and slides it under the table I'm setting up with plates and silverware.

"What guy?" I play dumb, hoping against hope that Louis stays on the other side of the rec center.

"The one staring you down and walking over here right now." *Double shit.*

I don't have time to respond before Louis wraps an arm around my waist and tries kissing me on the cheek. Immediately, my head turns so his mouth awkwardly lands in my hair.

"What do you think you're doing?" I try jerking out of his embrace, but his arm tightens around me.

"Greeting my girl," Louis answers, a smug smirk on his face.

"I'm not your girl."

"Aw, don't be like that, Sammy."

I hate it when he calls me Sammy. I'm Samantha, and Heath's best friend is Samuel. We don't go by shortened names so it doesn't get confusing. But even if Samuel didn't live around here, I still wouldn't like a nickname coming from Louis.

It reeks of intimacy, which is exactly what I don't want with him.

He attempts to lean in and kiss me again. But this time he's jerked back by a massive hand on the back of his collar. "Try that again, and you'll be drinking out of a straw for a month," Derek growls.

Normally, I don't condone the use of violence, but it's freaking hot to hear Derek defending me. All hard lines and feral energy.

I just barely contain the urge to fan myself.

"Who the hell are you?" Louis stares wide-eyed up at Derek, who has a few inches on the man.

"He's my boyfriend," I blurt out, seizing the opportunity to claim Derek as mine, even if it's not necessarily true.

"Nice try, Sammy. I know you're not dating anybody. You went to the Fall Harvest Dance alone, according to my mom. Same for the Christmas Gala. And the New Year's Bash."

Ugh, Mrs. Meeks. One of the biggest gossips in town.

And could Guardian Valley possibly have any more events for me to attend alone, where everyone and their literal moms could see and gossip?

"Your mom's misinformed. Derek wasn't available to accompany me those nights, but we are definitely together."

My hand slides up Derek's arm. His eyes are narrowed. His brow wrinkles as he considers the turn of events.

"Stop playing around, Sammy. I know you're not—"

I cut off his words with a hard kiss to Derek's mouth, lifting to my tiptoes to reach. As soon as our lips touch, everything outside the two of us becomes a distant hum. Louis's reaction. The murmurs of the volunteers around us. Everything else is inconsequential to this moment.

I'd worry about attacking Derek without consent, but his body immediately welcomes mine. His strong arms tugging me closer. His mouth opening so our tongues tangled together.

Good grief.

I never knew a kiss could feel like this. Granted, my experience is limited. *Hello, first kiss with the man plaguing me right now.* A ridiculously hopeful corner of my heart whispers that maybe this is my last first kiss.

Which is insanity.

Maybe I'm more like Heath than I thought. Because he fell for Adeline pretty fast, despite his initial denial.

Could I be falling for this scarred veteran? I barely know him. We've only had a few conversations. But there's something in him that calls to me.

Something elemental that can't be explained.

CHAPTER SIX

DEREK

"I'm not used to smiling very much."

SEVEN MINUTES IN HEAVEN.

That was the first and last time I kissed a girl.

It was junior year of high school and my buddy Chris invited me to the birthday party he was throwing while his parents were out of town. Like every horny teenage movie of the nineties and early aughts, the group agreed to play Seven Minutes in Heaven.

While I was nervous, a part of me was excited. Girls didn't flirt with me at school, but this game negated the immediate *no* I usually got once a girl spent more than a second looking at me.

Because during the game, we'd both be blindfolded in separate rooms and led to the infamous closet for our seven minutes. I figured if I made a good enough impression—no matter my inexperience—maybe my kissing skill would overcome my unattractiveness.

It hadn't worked. A naive sixteen-year-old's dream.

Madison Gardner put one hand on my cheek thirty seconds into the game and recoiled, immediately realizing who she was with. Game over for me.

But Samantha wasn't recoiling. She didn't seem to give a damn about my scarred flesh, her hands roaming over my cheek, neck, down to my chest, as she moaned into my mouth.

She only kissed me to get her douchebag ex off her back, but I don't care about her reasoning. I'm just pathetically thankful she chose me for her revenge.

This may be the only kiss I get from Samantha, but it's enough. Enough to wipe out Madison Gardner. Enough to erase the pitying looks of women in my past. All I can see and feel is Samantha. And I never want to lose that sensation.

When we finally break apart, both of us are breathing hard, our fingers digging into the other.

"Okay, okay... Break it up, you two." Mrs. Balducci, the rec center coordinator, shoves her way between the crowd of people ogling us. "Louis, leave this poor girl alone and go help Michael bring in more chairs from the storage closet. Derek, you come with me. We need an extra table for the empty corner over there. And Samantha, these tables aren't going to set themselves."

With her orders given, like a drill sergeant from my past Army days, everybody snaps to work. Samantha pats my chest with a shy smile before turning away to do as Mrs. Balducci says. Louis stalks off with a huff and I follow the older woman out to the hall.

"You're causing quite the stir, Mr. Housley."

"I'm sorry, ma'am."

"Oh, no need to apologize, and you can call me Helga. *Ma'am* makes me feel old." She taps the back of her pink hair. "I'm just happy to see Samantha with someone other than Louis."

"You don't like him?" I ask, desperate for more information about their past. When he'd claimed Samantha as his girl, I thought I might combust from the strength it took not to immediately knock the prick to the floor caveman-style.

"Oh, Louis is nice enough, I suppose, but he was never right for Samantha. You, on the other hand..." She eyes me speculatively as we stop at the end of the hall where a round table leans against the wall. "You think you can handle this by yourself, big guy? Or should I call for reinforcements?"

"I've got this, ma'am. I mean, Helga. You go see what else needs to be done."

"Thank you, dear. I knew I liked you. Samantha's got a good one." She winks and then toddles off. Her approval warms my chest, even if it doesn't necessarily matter.

Samantha only kissed me because Louis was there. It didn't mean anything, but I suppose on the off chance that it did, having a popular matron of Guardian Valley society on my side isn't a terrible thing.

On the ride home to the ranch two hours later, Samantha jumps into an explanation of her and Louis's relationship, and I'm relieved I didn't have to prompt her and reveal my intense curiosity.

"We dated a little in high school and then again last year, but each time I broke it off because I was never a priority."

"What do you mean?" It's unfathomable to me that a man could have Samantha in his life, in his arms, and choose *not* to spend time with her.

"He cared about everything else in his life more than me. In school, it was his studies and baseball. Now, it's his work and his recreational baseball team, even though it's the freakin' offseason. *February*." I can practically hear the roll of her eyes. "He forgot about me. Didn't think to invite me to work functions or hanging out with the team. Things like that. I wasn't really part of his life."

What a fucking idiot, and I say as much to Samantha. She laughs and the joyful sound makes me smile, stretching the tight skin of my cheeks. It's an uncomfortable but not unwelcome sensation.

I'm not used to smiling very much.

"I won't disagree with you. Heath basically said the same thing. I knew I shouldn't have given him a second chance last year, but you called it. I do get lonely here. Not many options as far as dating, especially when you've known everybody since you were in diapers."

"I can imagine."

"Did you grow up in a small town?"

Adjusting in my seat, my head shakes in the negative. "No. After my dad died, I bounced around between foster homes. Most of them were in the suburbs, but I never had enough time to put roots down to get to know people very well, let alone have them want to be part of my business. You were right about me earlier with the whole *no belonging* thing," I admit.

She tosses a quick nod of compassion my way. "It's a double-edged sword, that's for sure. I wouldn't want to float around life without something tethering me home, but it's also a nuisance when everybody knows everything about you. Are you at least close with your military friends?"

I shrug, looking out the window at the passing scenery. "We stay in touch, but I've always been a loner."

Samantha hums in her throat. "There's nothing wrong with not having a huge circle of friends, but you deserve a support system of people who care about you. Guess it's fortunate that now you have me, Heath, and Adeline, and the other three heirs when they show up."

"One big happy family." I joke.

"We could be, even if the other Foster heirs are terrible people, which I doubt. You'll still have three of us to count on, and that's more than you had before you came to Guardian Valley."

She has a point, but I've never really allowed myself to trust others when it came down to it. Mr. Foster's will only stipulated that I have to stay here for a year. When the twelve months are up, I'm free to go where I want.

Who knows if I'm going to stay in Guardian Valley, and if I don't, I'm sure Samantha, her brother, and his wife will forget about me soon after I'm gone.

The thought doesn't sit well.

CHAPTER SEVEN

SAMANTHA

*"You have permission to do whatever you want with me, baby.
You're calling the shots."*

I HATE THAT DEREK'S alone in the world.

Maybe I overstepped by volunteering my brother and sister-in-law as family, along with myself, but the matter-of-fact way Derek spoke about being a loner struck a chord in me.

I've always had friends. Knew people cared for me. Even though our mom died when we were young, our dad did his best to love Heath and I, and the rest of Guardian Valley helped.

But Derek didn't have a community to support him.

Until now.

I'll make sure of it.

Already he made headway with Mrs. Balducci by volunteering with me at the rec center. And Paige, a local high school teacher, shot me an approving look when Derek helped corral her little siblings while she worked on setting up the tables with me.

Except didn't Adeline mention the will only requires heirs to stay in Guardian Valley for a year? What if Derek decides to leave when his time is up?

A crazy idea more suited to a Lifetime Original movie pops into my head. Trapping him in town somehow. Tying us together in some way.

Girl, pull yourself together.

I may not be stalker/kidnapper level yet, but perhaps I should be more forthright about my feelings. Let him know where I stand, so he knows I'm serious about being there for him.

The gravel drive to Serenity Ranch comes into view, and I turn down the lane, driving past the main house until we're parked behind the last cabin before the property reverts back to wild land. We'll have privacy this far out since Heath and Levi, our other ranch hand, are staying in cabins closer to the house.

Ripping the keys out of the ignition, I toss them on the dash before twisting to face Derek. The truck has one long bench seat without a center console separating us, which is perfect for what I want to do.

"With all this talk of family, I feel like I should make one thing clear," I begin, scooting closer to brace a tentative hand on Derek's thigh. "Heath can be your brother, but I don't want to be your sister. Far from it."

"Is that right?" Derek's brows practically reach his jagged hairline at the announcement.

Swallowing hard against my suddenly dry throat, I nod. I've never been this bold with a man before. Never laid myself out on the line like this, and I never imagined I would for someone I've known for such a short time.

"If you let me, I'd like to be a whole heck of a lot more." I carefully watch his brown eyes as I lean closer, *closer*. Until my lashes flutter shut upon the touch of our lips.

This isn't the surprise kiss of earlier. That was hard, frenzied—a frantic attempt to grab as much pleasure as possible before he threw me away.

I don't think Derek's going to stop me, so we keep the kiss soft, searching, both of us slowly learning the other. He wraps his large hands around my waist and helps me settle on his lap, my thighs bracketing his.

"Is this okay?" he rasps.

In response, I reach down to start undoing his jeans. "I want you, Derek. I *need* you. Is *this* okay?" By now, my fingers have slid inside his boxers to grip his thick cock.

"Fuck, yes. You have permission to do whatever you want with me, baby. You're calling the shots." One of his hands grips my chin to make sure what he's saying is registering, our gazes clashing in heated understanding.

Free rein over Derek?

A rattle of nervous laughter threatens to bubble up, but I shove it down. Now's not the time to get cold feet. I initiated this. I need to finish it. *Finish* Derek. Because I'm desperate to erase that serious, unhappy expression he's been wearing since we first met.

Wiggling awkwardly, we manage to get my legging lowered, so I can kick them off over my converse. The entire thing took way longer than it should have because as soon as my violet cotton panties were revealed, Derek's fingers honed in on the soaked spot clinging to my pussy and refused to stop playing with it. Pushing it deeper in the crease, so he could tease my clit.

"I can't believe how wet you are for me," he murmurs, awe filling his gravelly voice.

"Have you seen yourself lately?" I say it without thinking, but the stiffening of Derek beneath me—and not in the good way—has me realizing my error. "Sorry, I didn't mean to bring up a sore spot for you. Your scars don't bother me. Frankly, I think they're sexy as hell. But I understand that was a traumatic time for you and—"

He shuts me up by dragging my lips to his. "No more talking about ugly things. Okay?"

I don't know if he's referring to the past or himself, and my heart breaks with how easily he believes he's ugly in any way.

Damn judgmental people.

I'm sure he's had his share of comments thrown his way. Even today at the rec center a couple of people stared until Mrs. Balducci kicked their asses into gear.

"Okay," I whisper, then carefully guide the tip of his cock to my pussy, shoving the wet cotton aside.

I sink lower into his lap and clench at the thickness stretching me down below. It feels so good, and we really haven't even started yet—just the brush of his cock sliding along my walls until I'm fully seated in his lap. My clit pressing to his pelvis.

It steals the breath from my lungs.

Derek's hands move from my waist down to clench my ass cheeks. "Fucking hell." He licks his lips before letting his head fall back on to the headrest, his eyes closing in pained pleasure.

I did that to him. This big, strong man is vibrating with barely leashed control beneath me, and I've never felt more powerful in my life.

Ex-boyfriend who?

None of our teenage fumbling or stilted touches last year compared to this. I doubt any man's touch would compare to the hypnotizing attraction of Derek.

"Something wrong?" I tease, rolling my hips like a freaking porn star. Arching my back. Tossing my hair over one shoulder. Utilizing the small space of the truck cab as much as I can.

"You know damn well you're fucking perfect. Trying to kill me with that tight as fuck pussy of yours."

I grin and continue grinding on him. The only thing that would make this better is if we were completely naked, and I could see all those glorious muscles of his like the first time I saw him chopping firewood.

Though with his insecurity about his scars, that'll probably be a battle in the future.

But it's not like I planned for us to fuck in this truck on the way back from volunteering, so I'll take what I can get.

And Derek's cock is more than enough for the taking.

CHAPTER EIGHT

DEREK

"I'm a man who's honed his control for years in the Army."

VIRGINITY IS OVERRATED.

I've always known it, despite the importance placed on the concept in a lot of the books I've read. Though rarely did those push virginity on the heroes. Make it a precious commodity.

Nope, the double standards were alive and well in some romances—not that I was judging. But I'm glad to finally be rid of mine, even if I never thought it'd be in a truck seat with a curvy woman who's determined to break through all of my walls.

"God, you're so thick..." Samantha moans again and her pussy clamps tighter around my hard length. If she keeps this up, I'm going to embarrass myself and come before she does, and that's unacceptable.

This may be my first time, but I'm no green boy. I'm a man who's honed his control for years in the Army. I can damn well control my dick until Samantha's writhing in pleasure from her orgasm.

Determined, I slip a hand between us and find her slick clit, toying with the sensitive flesh to learn what she likes. With each gasp and twitch of her pussy walls on my cock, I adjust the pressure of my fingers until Samantha's nails dig into my shoulders, her face burying itself into my hair, her hot breath teasing my ear.

"Don't stop... Please..."

"Don't worry, gorgeous, I like petting this sweet little clit too much to stop now. You're going to come on my dick like a good girl, then you're going to let me fill you up with my cum. Isn't that right?" All that dirty talk from books must have stuck in my brain because I've never talked to a woman like this before. Never understood the aphrodisiac of stuffing a woman full of my seed.

Until Samantha.

And my girl seems to crave it because she whimpers, driving herself deeper into my touch, her breasts squashed against my chest.

Next time she rides me, she's going to be topless so I can suck her nipples. The errant thought jets straight to my cock just as Samantha shouts my name, her palm slapping the fogged window and leaving a clear streak behind.

Her orgasm triggers mine, and together we shudder and groan, sweaty and replete in our new forged connection.

IN THE END, SAMANTHA got her way.

I moved into the main house that afternoon, and while I settled my things in a guest room, Samantha quickly made it clear that she expected me to stay in her room—in her bed—for the foreseeable future.

Heath grunted the next morning at breakfast upon learning of our new living situations, but he remained quiet until I joined him outside, away from Adeline and Samantha.

"You're both adults, so I'm trying not to treat Samantha like my kid sister who's still thirteen and wears braces, but just know that if I find out you've hurt her, we're going to have problems. Like you being buried in the back forty kind of problems. You got me?"

"I got you. Samantha knows she's in charge of whatever happens between us," I explain, hoping to ease some of his brotherly ire. I respect his need to protect his sister. It's the same need burning in me to ensure Samantha's happiness for as long as she'll let me.

I'm not quite delusional enough to think that'll mean forever, considering my history, but I'm willing to follow her lead.

"Great." Heath rolls his eyes then grins, slapping me on the shoulder. "She already thinks she runs this place, and now you're letting her run roughshod over you, too. I don't know if I should wish you luck or be thankful it's you who gets to deal with her stubbornness full-time rather than me."

Chuckling, we both head toward the stables where Heath's agreed to show me the ropes of the ranch. If I end up staying here longer than a year, I'll need to know more about how it runs than what end of a horse to avoid.

We spend a few hours outside until lunch arrives, and we split off—Heath heading toward his cottage shared with Adeline and me to the main house. As I round the corner, dust kicks up behind a black Charger racing down the drive.

I haven't been here long enough to know the comings and goings of visitors, but a part of me wonders if this could be another Foster heir.

Samantha seems to think we'll all become some sort of found family, but I have my doubts. Sure, we share a traumatic past—all of us losing our parents as children—but that doesn't mean we want to be pseudo-siblings. Or even friends.

Turns out I don't have to figure it out right now, though, because the man stepping out of the vehicle is definitely not a stranger.

It's fucking Louis.

Samantha's ex-boyfriend.

CHAPTER NINE

SAMANTHA

"Stop pretending like you're really into that fucking beast."

THERE'S AN INSISTENT knocking on the front door when I exit the bathroom wrapped in a giant fluffy towel. An entire jug of cold brew slipped through my fingers earlier and splashed all over me and the kitchen.

After cleaning up the mess, the usually comforting smell of coffee was giving me a headache, so I decided to take a shower to clean up.

And now I have a visitor.

I consider getting dressed real quick rather than answering the door practically naked, but the knocking gets louder. What if it's an emergency?

Accidents happen on the ranch all the time. What if someone is seriously wounded? What if it's Derek?

Panic constricts my lungs as I hurry downstairs and swing the door open.

Oh, shit. It's definitely not someone coming to tell me about an accident.

"What are you doing here, Louis?" My fingers go to the top of the towel and hold it tight, making sure the damn thing doesn't unravel.

"That's no way to greet an old friend, Sammy." He stares me up and down, and I cringe at the obvious desire in his eyes. "I came to see if you cooled down enough to cop to your lie at the rec center. If you're trying to make me jealous by inventing fake boyfriends, the least you can do is choose someone better than that ugly freak. A relationship between you two isn't believable at all. Though I think it's cute that you're trying so hard to catch my attention."

What the hell? Did we witness two different scenes yesterday?

"You must be out of your mind if you think I want you back. Derek and I are together, and I don't appreciate you insulting him. As far as I'm concerned, you're the ugly one—refusing to accept no as an answer, ignoring my boundaries."

"Drop the hard to get act. Everyone in town knows it's you and me in the end. Stop pretending like you're really into that fucking beast." Louis crosses his arms over his chest and shakes his head. Like somehow I'm disappointing him.

"That fucking beast warned you about bothering Samantha again." Derek steps onto the porch and I sigh in relief. I could've continued to handle Louis on my own; I've been taking care of myself for years.

But I like having Derek to back me up. Relish the warm feeling of safety and protection his presence blankets me in.

"Piss off. This is between me and Sammy."

"It's Samantha, asshole, and I'm not going anywhere." Derek looks to me over Louis's shoulder and adds, "Ever. I'm here for the long haul."

A thousand butterflies take off in my belly at his declaration. I wasn't expecting him to voice his commitment to me or Guardian Valley so soon after officially getting together, but I'll gladly accept it.

And I desperately want to seal the promise with his body relentlessly driving into mine.

We just have to get rid of Louis first.

But not in the Lifetime Original movie way, I inwardly chuckle.

"As for you..." Derek clamps a hand around Louis's arm and drags him down the steps like a rag doll, straight to the sleek Charger parked in front of the house. "Get lost and stay that way. I don't have any more time to waste on you because my girl needs my cock."

I gasp at the brazen way he just said that aloud, and my nipples peak beneath my towel.

He's not wrong, though.

Louis sputters in shock staring wide-eyed at Derek before attempting to look at me until my man blocks his view.

"You forfeited any right you had to see Samantha long ago. Now, get the fuck off this property before I kick your ass." Derek doesn't wait to see if Louis follows directions, instead he turns and marches back to me. Pushing me inside enough to slam the door closed and shove me against it, his mouth licking and sucking at the skin above my towel.

"What were you thinking about answering the door like this? Are you trying to get someone killed? I could've ripped that bastard's eyes out for seeing your sexy little body overflowing this scrap of fabric."

"It's more than a scrap," I correct. It's the largest one I own because my body's too curvy for regular-sized towels.

"You're dripping wet. Fucking glistening under the sunlight," he continues as if I hadn't spoken. "And you thought you should talk to that prick while he got to see what's mine? Oh, baby, I don't think so."

This time I don't bother responding. It's obvious Derek's too flustered and in his own head to listen to any excuse I give him. Not that I'm particularly inclined to.

This feral beast running his hands and mouth over my needy body is sexy as hell.

"I'll show you who you belong to," he grits out, lowering to his knees. His hands rip the towel off me and toss it aside before spreading my thighs wider.

Air barely has time to cool my heated flesh before Derek buries his face into my pussy, lapping at my clit with firm strokes as his thick fingers drive forward and find my G-spot.

"Oh my god!" I shout, the onslaught too much. Derek admitted last night when we were snuggled in my bed that he'd been a virgin, which I'm pretty sure means this is his first time going down on a woman.

Not that I'd know. This is the first time anyone's eaten me out, and Derek's doing a damn good job of it.

"You taste so fucking good, baby. I thought I loved your baked goods, but you were hiding the sweetest part of you this whole time."

I blush at his words but arch into his mouth, asking for more with quiet abandon.

Derek doesn't need much encouragement. He growls and the vibrations make me jump, but his free hand presses on the center of my chest to keep me pinned to the door.

"Come for me, Samantha. I need your juicy pussy to soak my lips and chin with your pleasure. Need this pretty cunt nice and soft so I can fuck you deep with my big cock."

"Yes... Derek!" My body obeys his demand, and the tension outlining my muscles snaps, the orgasm blinding me with its power.

I slump against the door as Derek gently kisses his way up my tingling body. A tickle of my belly button. A nibble of my breast.

It all leads to his lips finding mine right as he lifts me in his arms and drops me onto his steel cock.

"Derek!"

"I warned you, baby. Nice and soft, so you can take me deep and milk me with that hot pussy." He thrusts roughly into me, shoving me further up the door at my back.

I fucking love it.

I'm not a light girl and being held aloft, used for Derek's pleasure as he plunges deeper, harder... Well, it's what my fantasies have been made of. Especially since I first caught my pseudo-lumberjack shirtless.

As we both groan in relief with our combined pleasure, I know I'm never going to forget that moment.

Or this one.

Because the first time was when I met the man of my dreams, and the second was when he accepted me as his woman.

For good.

EPILOGUE

DEREK

"Count on Samantha to heal what parts of me she could."

THE DOORBELL RINGS and I raise a hand as Samantha goes to answer it.

"I've got it. Just make sure she doesn't cheat." I direct the warning to Heath who nods.

The four of us are playing Monopoly and my girl is cutthroat. She likes to win. Which is hilarious and adorable. And absolutely not going to happen if I have any say in the matter.

Because I like to win, too.

Another smile stretches my scars but it's getting easier, less noticeable. I guess using those muscles more really does make a difference.

Count on Samantha to heal what parts of me she could.

After unlocking the front door, it swings open harder than I intended with an icy breeze. Damn, it's cold here. Montana is a world away from my mostly southern living.

A young woman stands on the porch, a red suitcase by her side, and she offers a shy smile. "Hi, I'm Brooke. Mr. Foster's attorney said I could stay here?"

Curious about Brooke's arrival in Guardian Valley? Don't miss her romance with a certain surprise neighbor next in *Montana Savior*! Turn the page for a sneak peek at the first chapter!

CHAPTER ONE

TRAVIS GIBSON

"He had no right to touch you."

OWNING A NIGHTCLUB is a real bitch sometimes.

Aside from working odd hours, patrons can be straight-up assholes who assume they're God's gift to humanity and deserve to be treated as such. My staff knows how to handle these kinds of customers—quickly, efficiently, and without drama—so why the hell am I inserting myself into a situation where I don't belong?

Because from the moment I spotted the gorgeous woman draped in blue satin step into The Charleston Cellar, I haven't been able to take my eyes off her.

As the CEO of a conglomerate of upscale lounges around the country, beautiful women frequenting my business aren't an anomaly. Tall, short, thin, round. I've seen them all. Been attracted to many of them. And while at forty years of age I rarely indulge that attraction with guests, my younger self hadn't been as discerning.

So, in theory, this woman shouldn't have caught my attention and held it for the past hour. Nor should a wave of protectiveness have propelled me forward once I saw a man at the bar touch her bare back.

Yet here I am with my hand wrapped around the bastard's wrist, tempted to snap it backward in a painful break if not for the woman's fearful gaze and my bouncer's stern look of reproach.

"Mr. Gibson, I'll take it from here," Jared says, settling a firm hand on the man's shoulder and forcefully guiding him away from the curious crowd watching our altercation.

"You're going to let him get away with that?" An indignant protest rises from the man as he tries to get free of Jared. "He could've broken my wrist!"

"But I didn't. Pity, since it's what you deserve."

He glances back at Jared. "He just threatened me! Do you know who I am? My father is George Hildebrand, and I demand to be released. That maniac should be kicked out, not me!"

Jared and I share a look over the guy's head. There's always a rich prick shouting about his powerful daddy. The sad part is it isn't always college kids either. Grown adults, like this man who doesn't look much younger than me, use their wealthy parents as a protective shield, too.

"This really isn't necessary." A small hand tentatively tugs on my sleeve, and I face the woman at the center of this debacle. Embarrassment and guilt flush her cheeks red. Dark pupils eclipse the bright blue of her eyes.

"It is." My hand covers hers and draws it into mine to massage the palm with my thumb. "He had no right to touch you."

Neither do I, but I've never considered myself a 'good' man. It's tough building a business in New York City. Tougher still when you start at the bottom with no connections and even less cash. But I scraped and clawed my way to the top of a luxurious entertainment empire, so now money and connections lay at my feet like sycophants, though an annoying emptiness still gnaws at the edges of my life.

And with each new club I open, it only burrows deeper rather than disappearing. I've become a cliché about the wealthy businessman unsatisfied with his golden lifestyle.

"We told you the guys would be all over you in that dress." The woman behind her grins. "You're irresistible, Brooke."

"I agree." The low murmur is only meant for Brooke's ears, and I know she heard me when the tips of her ears turn pink. "Why don't I take you somewhere more private for a breather. Let everyone calm down without having you to focus on."

The crowd of onlookers still hasn't dissipated, and once Brooke notices, her gaze bounces between me and her friend.

"You got some ID on you, big guy?"

Pulling out my wallet, I let the woman snap a picture of my license before she shoos us away. "I'm going to wait for Adeline to get back, then fill her in. You get some fresh air, hon... It'll do you good."

I don't know why Brooke's friend is so gungho for us to hang out alone, but I'm not going to question it. She's got my name and address if anything goes sideways, not that I'd ever harm a woman, let alone the curvy one I've had my sights on all evening.

"Um, okay." Brooke peeks shyly up at me through her lashes, and I use my hold on her hand to tug her behind me through the mass of people dancing and drinking.

With a swift ascent to my office, we're soon locked away in a private cocoon overlooking the club below. The special windows allow us to look down on the crowd without them being able to see us.

Reluctantly, I release her hand and head toward the bar across from my desk. Maybe a little alcohol will help Brooke relax because right now all I see are nerves radiating from her pores like a bunny run to ground.

"There's nothing to worry about. I don't bite." *Unless asked.* "My name's Travis Gibson, and I own this club. It's my duty to take care of all my guests and see to their comfort and safety."

Perhaps not to this extreme, but she doesn't need to know that.

"Brooke Stanley." She thanks me as I offer a tumbler of brandy. Her face pinches at the taste, and I bite the inside of my cheek in an effort not to laugh at the adorably innocent reaction.

"So, Brooke Stanley," her name rolls off my tongue, simple and sweet, "what brings you to The Charleston Cellar? Girls' night out?"

Nodding, she licks her lips, immediately drawing my attention to the glistening bow of her mouth. I shift to the side as we both stare out the windows—my cock swelling at the image of her plump lips circling the tip, her eyes holding my gaze as if waiting for approval.

Damn. I swallow the entire glass of expensive liquor with no thought toward savoring it. Brooke on her knees for me would be a hell of a sight.

"We're celebrating my last night in New York."
What?

In sixth grade, I got in my first fist fight. Johnny Levinson laughed at the haircut my mom gave me, so I decked him in the jaw. A haphazard brawl broke out between us, and Johnny landed a punch to my gut.

That's how Brooke's declaration feels.

Like the wind has been knocked out of me—my stomach twisted in a knot.

"Oh?" My tone conveys none of my inner turmoil. A skill honed across decades of hiding my true emotions before someone chose to take advantage. Viewing them as a weakness.

Come to think of it, my neutral mask began forming not too long after that fight in sixth grade. Too many bullies found pleasure in making a poor trailer park kid's life hell. Mom was already overworked and running on fumes. Patching my split lips and black eyes only wore her down more.

So I learned to control myself.

Learned not to react. Outwardly, at least.

It's served me well in life and business.

Brooke nods and sweeps a curl behind her ear. "Adeline and Samantha came to help me with movers and everything before our flight back to Montana tomorrow."

Fucking Montana?

This time, I couldn't stop the grinding of my teeth at her casual announcement.

I may not look like the typical Montanan with my three-piece suits, Aston Martin, and penthouse overlooking Central Park, but it's where I grew up. Where I began my journey to the top of the corporate world, despite humble beginnings.

"Big Sky Country," I murmur, listing the one detail people tend to list when they hear Montana. "Is that where you're from originally?"

"Close... Just a little more west. Boise, Idaho. But Guardian Valley will be home now."

I cover a cough of shock with my fist. So much for my legendary control. Brooke's shattered it with a well-placed tap of her pink-tipped nail.

Because my business partner and I just bought land in Guardian Valley. An idyllic estate meant to wipe out all the bad memories of my past.

What are the fucking odds?

Sounds like sparks will soon be flying...
Find out what happens next in *Montana Savior*!

THANKS FOR READING & DON'T FORGET TO RATE/ REVIEW!

Please consider leaving a rating/review. Ratings & reviews are the #1 way to support an indie author like me.
The more reviews, the more my books are shown to other potential readers! And they serve as guides to readers on whether or not to take a chance on an indie author.
I appreciate your support!
XO, Hallie

ABOUT THE AUTHOR

Hallie prefers steamy, insta-love stories where curvy girls are claimed by filthy-talking heroes. And when she ran out of reading material, she decided to write her own stories. If you want a quick, hot read, she's your girl!

Find more about Hallie Bennett HERE[1]!

---

1. https://www.thearrowedheart.com/hallie-bennett